AF269755

Table of Contents

Can you find these words?

Congress

democracy

freedom

government

Capitol Building
A symbol stands for an idea.
3

The Capitol Building is a symbol
of **democracy**.

It is a symbol of **freedom**.

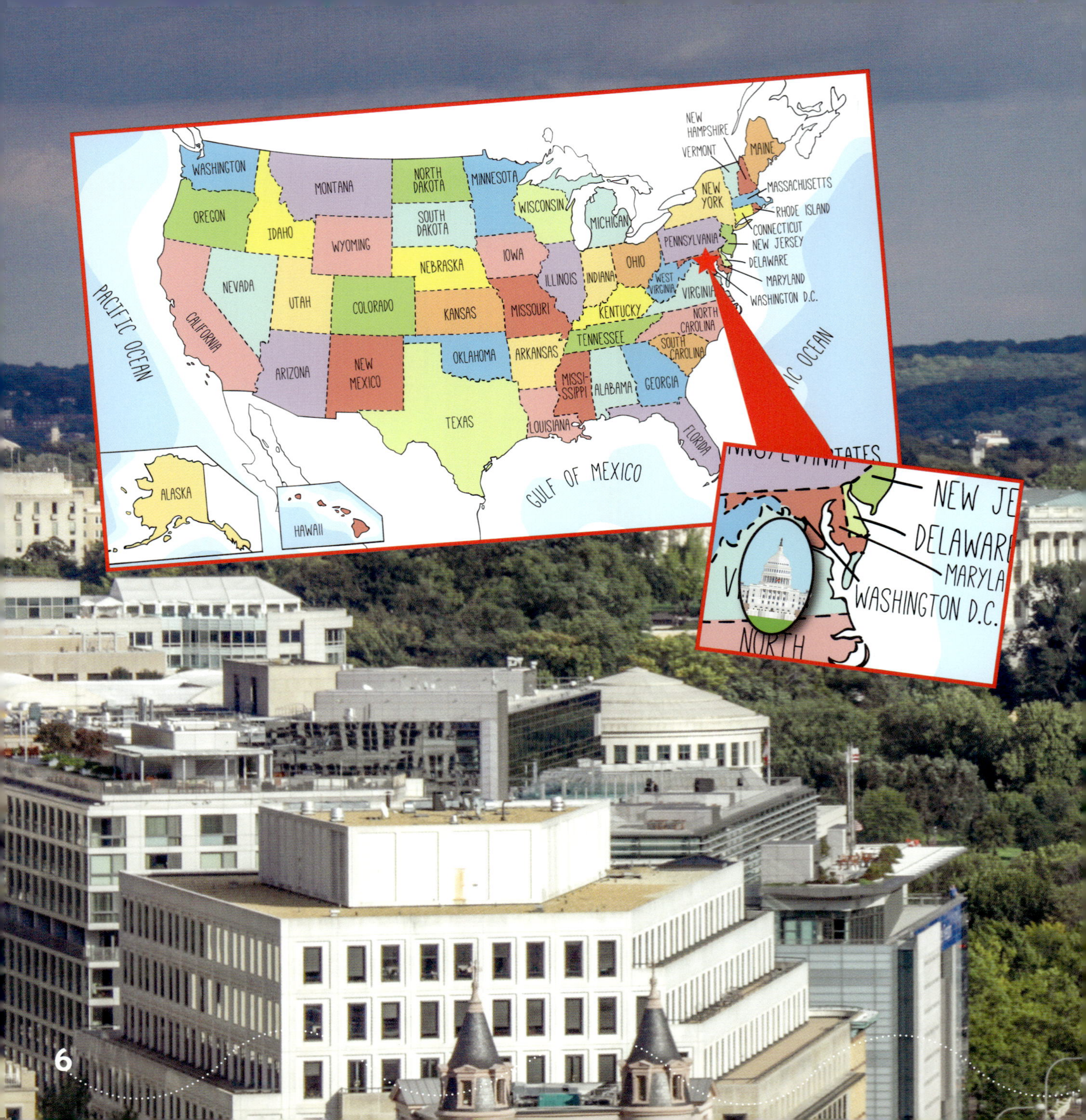

PACIFIC OCEAN
WASHINGTON
OREGON
MONTANA
NORTH DAKOTA
MINNESOTA
IDAHO
WYOMING
SOUTH DAKOTA
WISCONSIN
MICHIGAN
NEVADA
UTAH
COLORADO
NEBRASKA
IOWA
ILLINOIS
INDIANA
OHIO
CALIFORNIA
ARIZONA
NEW MEXICO
KANSAS
MISSOURI
KENTUCKY
WEST VIRGINIA
VIRGINIA
OKLAHOMA
ARKANSAS
TENNESSEE
NORTH CAROLINA
SOUTH CAROLINA
TEXAS
LOUISIANA
MISSISSIPPI
ALABAMA
GEORGIA
FLORIDA
ALASKA
HAWAII
GULF OF MEXICO
NEW HAMPSHIRE
VERMONT
MAINE
NEW YORK
MASSACHUSETTS
RHODE ISLAND
CONNECTICUT
NEW JERSEY
PENNSYLVANIA
DELAWARE
MARYLAND
WASHINGTON D.C.
NEW JE
DELAWARE
MARYLA
WASHINGTON D.C.
NORTH

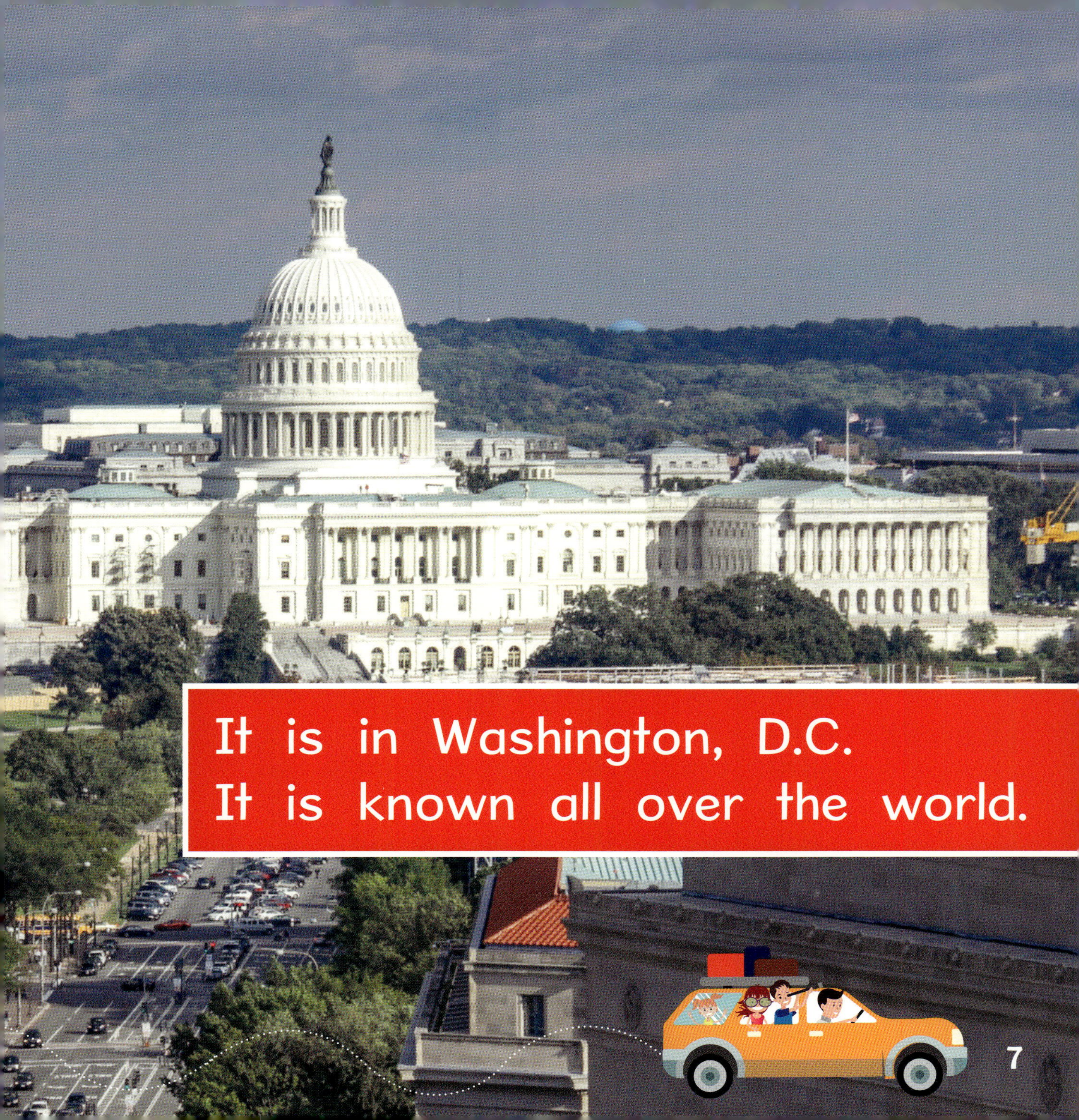

It is in Washington, D.C.
It is known all over the world.

The Statue of Freedom stands at the top.

It wears a helmet.
It holds a sword.

Congress members meet here.

New laws are made here.

People visit the Capitol Building every day.

They take tours. They watch the **government** work.

Did you find these words?

Congress members meet here.

The Capitol Building is a symbol of **democracy**.

It is a symbol of **freedom**.

They watch the **government** work.

Photo Glossary

Congress (KAHNG-gris): The law-making body of the United States.

democracy (di-MAH-kruh-see): A form of government that allows the people to choose their leaders in elections.

freedom (FREE-duhm): The ability to do or say whatever you want.

government (GUHV-urn-muhnt): The group of people who govern a state or country.

Index

About the Author

K.A. Robertson is a writer and editor who enjoys learning about the history of the United States. She first visited the Capitol Building as a teenager. It is one of her favorite places!

www.rourkeeducationalmedia.com

PHOTO CREDITS: Cover: ©tupungato; p2,10,14,15: ©NASA/Bill Ingalls; p2,4,14,15: lucky-photographer; p2,5,14,15: ©rzdeb; p2,12,14,15: ©TriggerPhoto; p3: ©Jason Doiy; p6,7: ©dkfielding; p8: ©rararorro; p9: ©Stephen Emlund

Edited by: Keli Sipperley
Cover: Rhea Magaro-Wallace
Interior Layout: Corey Mills

Library of Congress PCN Data
Capitol Building / K.A. Robertson
(Visiting U.S. Symbols)
ISBN 978-1-64369-058-2 (hard cover)(alk. paper)
ISBN 978-1-64369-120-6 (soft cover)
ISBN 978-1-64369-205-0 (e-Book)
Library of Congress Control Number: 2018955826

Printed in the United States of America, North Mankato, Minnesota